Published in the United States by Random House, Inc., New York, and simultaneously in Canada by Random House of Canada Limited, Toronto, in conjunction with Sesame Workshop.
Library of Congress Cataloging-in-Publication Data
Lukas, Sarah. Hand in hand in Dragon Land / by Sarah Lukas ; illustrated by Ted Enik ; based on the characters by Ron Rodecker.
p. cm. "Dragon tales." "A sparkle storybook."
SUMMARY: Max and Emmy make a wish on a magic scale and are carried to Dragon Land, where they have a picnic, play with their dragon friends, and visit Quetzal's garden.
ISBN 0-375-81443-4
[1. Dragons—Fiction. 2. Magic—Fiction. 3. Stories in rhyme.]
I. Enik, Ted, ill. II. Rodecker, Ron. III. Title.
PZ8.3.A3295 Han 2002 [E]—dc21 2001019279
www.randomhouse.com/kids/sesame
Visit Dragon Tales on the Web at www.dragontales.com
Printed in Italy April 2002 10 9 8 7 6 5 4 3 2 1

Hand in Hand in Dragon Land

I wish, I wish
With all my heart
To fly with dragons
In a land apart.

By Sarah Lukas
Illustrated by Ted Enik
Based on the characters by Ron Rodecker

RANDOM HOUSE NEW YORK

Peek in this playroom and, in a secret space,
Spy a dragon scale from a faraway place.
Max and Emmy understand
The secret to get to Dragon Land.
They make a wish on the magic scale
And it whisks them there in a starry trail.

Come along and visit, too!
Your dragon friends are calling you!

Look! A magical place where dragons walk,
Where fountains sing and flowers talk.
We'll cannonball into Dragoon Lagoon
And eat dragonberry jam with a sparkly spoon.

What is that sound? It's a growly grumbling.
If there's food around, it's Ord's tummy rumbling.

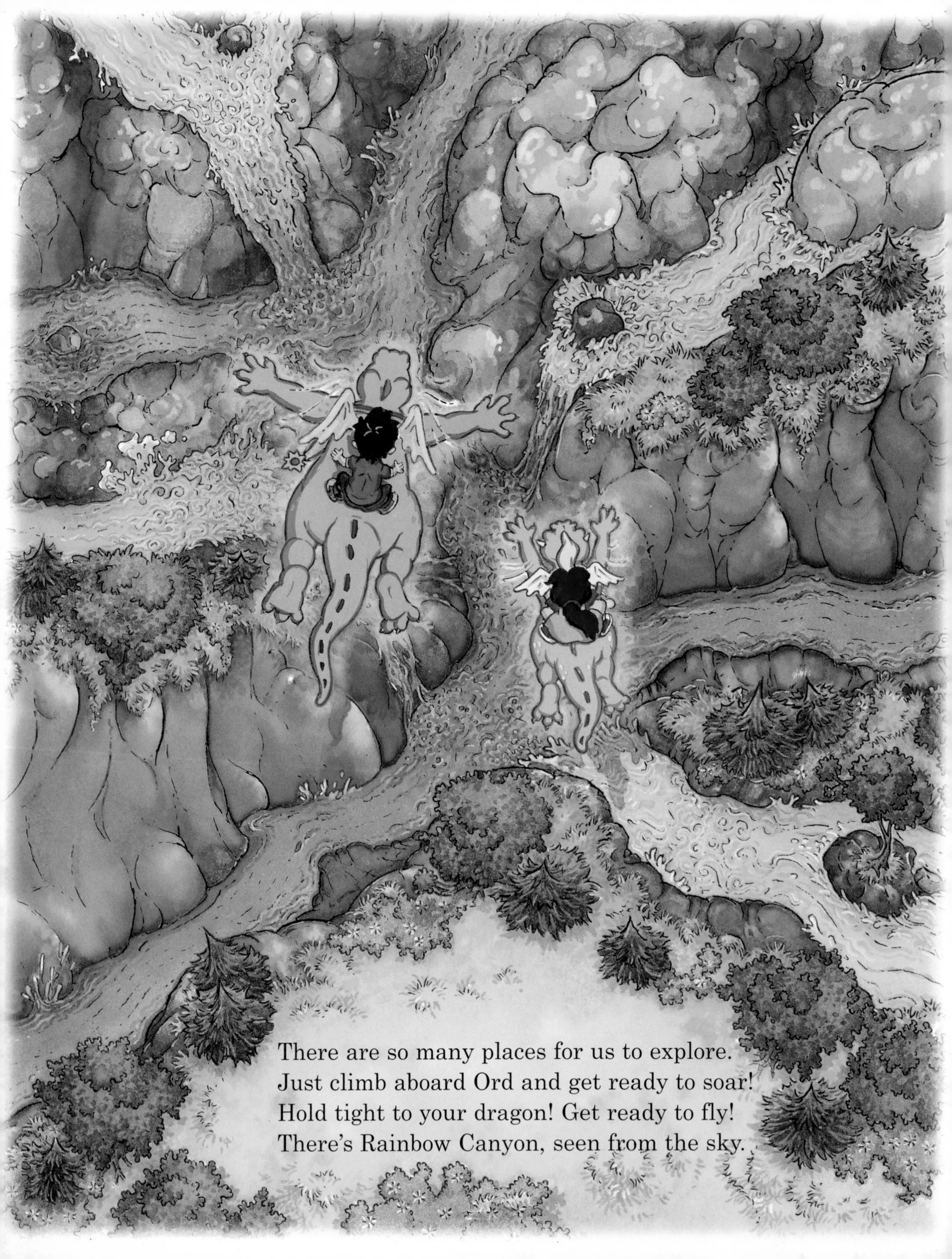

There are so many places for us to explore.
Just climb aboard Ord and get ready to soar!
Hold tight to your dragon! Get ready to fly!
There's Rainbow Canyon, seen from the sky.

Let's collect all the colors! We'll play in the sun.
When the rain falls, colors blend into one.

What's going on in the field today?
It's a dragonball game, and they need you to play!
Do you want Zak and Wheezie to join in the game?
Find a knuckerhole then, and call them by name!

Zak likes things tidy; he flies slow and easy.
Not like his sister, the wild, wacky Wheezie.

A back flip! Some somersaults! A *boing* and a *spring*!
"Mushroom Meadow," says Max, "is the bounciest thing!"

Pfefferthistle flowers have thistle sap that's sticky.
Try to say *that* ten times fast. It gets pretty tricky!

In the songflower patch you'll see flutterbies fly.
Follow them up, up, up to the School in the Sky.

Cassie is smart and thoughtful and kind.
Her badge will shine when she speaks her mind.

Quetzal, the teacher, is ancient and sage.
In his Big Storybook, pictures dance off the page.
"*¡Hola, niños!*" says Quetzal. (He's from Mexico.)
"Bundle up warm, *pequeños*, and then off you go!"

"I see you have brought some new friends.
¡Que bueno!"
Do you think Quetzal means *you*?
I suspect so!

Past the Rag-na-Rock caves and a musical fountain,
High on the peaks of Stickleback Mountain,
There is always a billowy blanket of snow
Just perfect for sledding—but watch out below!
Down the powdery slopes, Zak and Wheezie's sled zings.
They'll fly you back up if you haven't got wings.

Go ’round Dandelion Forest—try not to fly through,
Or those fierce dandelions just might growl at you!

Cassie knows a quieter place to play.
Point your nose to the sky, and we'll fly that way!

The Playground in the Sky has new things to ride.
There's a drum trampoline and a xylophone slide!
Emmy rocks on a horse. Cassie swings just above it.
Max swoops on some monkey bars. Wheezie sings,

"Looooove it!"

Just past Turtle Rock the light starts to fade.
It's the Forest of Darkness, where Ord feels afraid.
But it has to be dark so the Star Tree will glow.
So will Ord's dragon badge in the shadows below.

In his garden, Quetzal's tending unusual flowers,
Like dipsy-doo daisies and loll-lily towers.

Come sniff the sweet blossoms—and then hear them giggle!
See jugglebugs juggle and jitterbugs jiggle.
Taste berries, see fairies who greet you with doodles.
Gently touch a clutch of tickly caterpoozles.

The dragons loved having you here to play.
Now to get back home, here's what you say:
"I wish, I wish, to use this rhyme
To go back home until next time."

If you want
to come back
and are
wondering
when,
Well, just open
the book--
and start over
again...